Samuel French Acting Edition

Wink

by Jen Silverman

ı|SAMUEL FRENCHı|ı

SAMUELFRENCH.COM   SAMUELFRENCH.CO.UK

For all enquiries regarding motion picture, television, and other media rights, please contact Samuel French.

MUSIC USE NOTE

Licensees are solely responsible for obtaining formal written permission from copyright owners to use copyrighted music in the performance of this play and are strongly cautioned to do so. If no such permission is obtained by the licensee, then the licensee must use only original music that the licensee owns and controls. Licensees are solely responsible and liable for all music clearances and shall indemnify the copyright owners of the play(s) and their licensing agent, Samuel French, against any costs, expenses, losses and liabilities arising from the use of music by licensees. Please contact the appropriate music licensing authority in your territory for the rights to any incidental music.

IMPORTANT BILLING AND CREDIT REQUIREMENTS

If you have obtained performance rights to this title, please refer to your licensing agreement for important billing and credit requirements.

WINK premiered at Marin Theatre Company in Mill Valley, California in June 2019 under the artistic leadership of Jasson Minadakis. The production was directed by Mike Donahue, with set and costume design by Dane Laffrey, lighting design by Jen Schriever, sound design by Jake Rodriguez, song composition by Daniel Kluger, and dramaturgy by Laura Brueckner. The cast was as follows:

SOFIE . . . . .Liz Sklar

GREGOR . . . . .Seann Gallagher

WINK . . . . .John William Watkins

DR. FRANS . . . . Kevin R. Free

CHARACTERS

SOFIE – (F) Dissatisfied in her marriage. Her cat has gone missing.

GREGOR – (M) Her husband. He skinned the cat.

WINK – (M) The cat. Lithe, dangerous, sensuous.

DR. FRANS – (M) A psychologist. Doctor to both Sofie and Gregor. A deeply lonely man.

SETTING

Wherever you are.

TIME

Now-ish, and simultaneously then-ish.

AUTHOR'S NOTES

On Notation:
[ ] is not spoken, although the character is thinking it.
/ signifies an interruption.

On Casting:
Characters can be played by actors of any ethnicity. This should go without saying, but please avoid a scenario in which all three humans are played by white actors and the cat is an actor of color.

While Dr. Frans, Gregor, and Wink are male characters and Sofie is a female character, these roles are open to genderqueer, transgender, and gender non-conforming actors.

On Space, Speed, and Transitions:
This play moves quickly, inexorably forward. Actors should think on the lines – this is not a world where characters have a great deal of time to consider anything before they do it. To those ends: transitions should take as little time as possible. If the energy slows or sags in transitions, we lose the headlong plunge that is so vital to this play.

In the first production we found that it made sense for the same space to represent both Sofie and Gregor's house and Dr. Frans' office. There are other ways to imagine the set, of course, but the overarching principle for all design choices should be speed, simplicity, and immediacy.

On Tone:

All of the characters are wrestling – in their own ways – with the darkness and the weight of their lives. All of them are desperately sincere, no matter how strange their escalating decisions become. The play should be performed in whatever your normal accent is.

Special Thanks:

Special thanks to the following people and institutions, who came to this play at pivotal moments along the way and were integral to its development: Jeremy Cohen and the Playwrights' Center, Marsha Norman and Juilliard, Jessi D. Hill and terraNOVA Collective, New Dramatists, Rose Riordan and Portland Center Stage, Kimberly Colburn, Ken Rus Schmoll, Dito Van Reigersberg, Birgit Huppuch, Andrew Garman, Anthony Skuse, and of course Marin Theatre Company and the company of collaborators who premiered it there.

1.

(Gregor and Sofie's home. **GREGOR** *wears a suit. He attempts to read the newspaper and enjoy his post-work drink as* **SOFIE** *roams the space.)*

SOFIE. Where's my cat?

GREGOR. Your what?

SOFIE. My cat.

GREGOR. I don't know. How could I know?

SOFIE. It's been two days.

GREGOR. Cats are mysterious.

SOFIE. He's an indoor cat.

GREGOR. Cats are loners.

SOFIE. He's not a loner.

GREGOR. Cats are uncommunicative. They vanish, they return.

SOFIE. You are uncommunicative and I still know where you are every second.

GREGOR. I'm sure that Wink is all right.

SOFIE. I know you hate him.

GREGOR. I don't hate your cat.

SOFIE. Say his name.

GREGOR. What?

SOFIE. Say it.

GREGOR. This is ridiculous.

SOFIE. Say it.

GREGOR. "Wink." Okay?

SOFIE. Again.

GREGOR. Wink Wink Wink the cat.

SOFIE. I can hear it.

I can hear in your voice how much you hate him.

GREGOR. I don't hate him. I don't hate anybody. I don't even believe in hate.

SOFIE. I'm going in your study.

GREGOR. He's not in my study.

SOFIE. You should check at the office.

GREGOR. THE CAT is not at my place of WORK, Sofie.

SOFIE. I need him. I need Wink.

GREGOR. I don't know where your cat is.

2.

(The office of **DR. FRANS**. **GREGOR** *reclines on his leather couch.)*

GREGOR. I skinned the cat.

DR. FRANS. I see.

GREGOR. With scissors.

DR. FRANS. I see.

GREGOR. I couldn't use the knives.

DR. FRANS. And why is that?

GREGOR. Sofie has become a vegetarian. She cooks with those knives.

DR. FRANS. That was very thoughtful of you.

GREGOR. Thank you.

DR. FRANS. Do you feel better now that you have skinned the cat?

GREGOR. I think I do. Yes. It's hard to tell. But yes.

DR. FRANS. How do you feel?

GREGOR. Right after the event – I felt as if I had a new lease on life. A great liberty. A ringing – clarity, if you will. I walked out on the balcony. I took several deep breaths. The city was so bright! The sunlight was so – light! The air! It was very airlike.

DR. FRANS. This is good, this is very good.

GREGOR. I looked at my hands. They appeared to be hands.

DR. FRANS. Yes yes, wonderful.

GREGOR. There was blood, of course.

DR. FRANS. That is natural.

GREGOR. And hair.

DR. FRANS. One cannot skin a cat without a little hair.

GREGOR. So: that is how it was.

DR. FRANS. I congratulate you.

And how was the experience for your wife?

GREGOR. What experience?

DR. FRANS. Your interaction with the cat.

GREGOR. Well.

DR. FRANS. Yes?

GREGOR. You see.

DR. FRANS. Yes, go on.

GREGOR. I have not told her.

DR. FRANS. So you have non-consensually skinned this cat.

GREGOR. I am afraid so, yes.

DR. FRANS. It was not agreed upon beforehand, not a reconfiguration of the values of your home?

GREGOR. It stinks, this cat, it scratches. It has eyes like a goat. I skinned it.

DR. FRANS. Hmm.
And what did you do with it after you skinned it?

GREGOR. I buried it in the garden.

DR. FRANS. *(Disapproving.)* Hmm.

GREGOR. And then I threw away my gloves. I put away the shovel.
And I went to work.

DR. FRANS. *(More brightly.)* Ah!
And how is work?

GREGOR. Depressing, it fills me with depression.

DR. FRANS. Normal! That is very normal.

GREGOR. I am depressed at work, and then I come home and I am depressed at home.

DR. FRANS. Better that than to suffer an enormity of feeling.

GREGOR. I'm sure you're right.

DR. FRANS. Perhaps you and Sofie should go on a vacation.

GREGOR. A vacation?

DR. FRANS. The two of you could be alone together.

GREGOR. What would we talk about?

DR. FRANS. Public health in the developing world?

GREGOR. ...There is one other matter. Regarding the cat.

DR. FRANS. I think it is best to move on from the cat.

GREGOR. I cannot, I cannot yet move on from the cat.

I – you see. The fact is.

I have kept the skin.

DR. FRANS. The skin.

GREGOR. In a box.

DR. FRANS. In a *box*.

GREGOR. Out of sight.

DR. FRANS. Ah. Hmm.

GREGOR. And at night. When I can't sleep.

I take out this box.

And I open it. And I look inside.

DR. FRANS. And how do you feel?

GREGOR. I feel…aroused.

DR. FRANS. Aroused?

GREGOR. Strangely aroused.

DR. FRANS. Ah!

GREGOR. Is it normal?

DR. FRANS. No. No, it is not normal.

GREGOR. Is it perhaps connected to my childhood?

DR. FRANS. I doubt it.

GREGOR. Or my parents, the values they instilled in me –?

DR. FRANS. No…no, that seems unlikely.

GREGOR. What do you think it means?

DR. FRANS. This was a male cat, was it not?

GREGOR. Yes.

DR. FRANS. And you are a man, are you not?

GREGOR. Yes, yes…

DR. FRANS. You are displaying latent homosexual tendencies, Gregor.

GREGOR. I am?

DR. FRANS. I am sorry to say it, but you are.

GREGOR. That's terrible. That's disheartening. What can I do?

DR. FRANS. You must dig the cat up.

GREGOR. Dig him up!

DR. FRANS. You must dig him up from the garden at a time when Sofie is not at home. And you must hold him against your chest, his skinless body, and as all of your darkest, crudest, most bestial impulses rise to the surface, Gregor, you must SLAM THEM BACK DOWN.

GREGOR. Slam –?

DR. FRANS. SLAM THEM DOWN.

GREGOR. Slam them...DOWN.

DR. FRANS. SLAM THEM DOWN!

GREGOR. SLAM THEM DOWN!

DR. FRANS. SLAM THEM DOWN!!

GREGOR. SLAM THEM DOWN!!

DR. FRANS & GREGOR. SLAM THEM DOWN!!!!

> *(Both men regain control of their breathing.)*
>
> *(They were really into it. They look away.)*

DR. FRANS. And after you have – slammed down – these impulses, you may rebury the cat. And as you do, you must say to yourself, "I am a man who has slammed down my darkest impulses with the light of civilization."

GREGOR. "I am a man –"

DR. FRANS. – And then you must take Sofie on vacation. That is my best advice for you.

I think we have reached time.

> *(**GREGOR** gets up to go. In the door:)*

GREGOR. Doctor?

DR. FRANS. What is it.

GREGOR. What if the thing I am feeling, the impulse rising to the top as I hold Wink's skinned fur in my own two hands – what if the thing rising up in me is *not* a latent homosexual tendency at all, but rather an electric awareness of my own capacity for violence and my desire to repeat those violent acts again and again in greater and greater volume?

> *(Long beat.)*

DR. FRANS. I doubt that that is the case, Gregor.

GREGOR. Oh. All right.

(He leaves.)

3.

(**DR. FRANS**' *office.* **SOFIE** *perches on his couch.
She is distraught.*)

SOFIE. I am distraught without Wink.

DR. FRANS. I see.

SOFIE. I can't eat. I can't sleep. I can't concentrate.

DR. FRANS. Oh dear...

SOFIE. I want to do terrible things to people who look like
they're happy.

DR. FRANS. *(This isn't so bad...)* Hmm...

SOFIE. A child laughed in front of me at the grocery store
and I wanted to end its life.

DR. FRANS. *(A little brighter.)* Well that's normal.

SOFIE. Oh.

That's good.

How was Gregor's session?

DR. FRANS. You know I cannot discuss –

SOFIE. Did he say anything about Wink?

DR. FRANS. Sofie.

SOFIE. Did he say anything maybe about if he wasn't careful
and left a window open or maybe the door or maybe –?

DR. FRANS. We are here to talk about you, Sofie.

How are *you* feeling?

SOFIE. Sad.

DR. FRANS. Ah...

SOFIE. Murderously sad.

DR. FRANS. Hmm.

SOFIE. I wake up. I dress. There is cat fur in my hair brush.
There is cat fur on my clothes. I drink coffee. I remove
cat fur from the inside of my mouth. I weep. I imagine
ripping out my own heart, placing it on the table, and
watching it slowly, finally, cease beating.

DR. FRANS. And how have you been recovering?

SOFIE. Recovering?

DR. FRANS. Yes, recovering.

SOFIE. Well.

DR. FRANS. Yes?

SOFIE. You see.

I have *not* been recovering.

DR. FRANS. One must recover, Sofie.

SOFIE. One must?

DR. FRANS. The world is a terrible and abrupt place. Terrible things happen abruptly.

It is our job to recover.

SOFIE. Oh.

Well.

How...does one recover?

DR. FRANS. Have you tried housework?

SOFIE. Housework is depressing.

DR. FRANS. Normal! That is very normal.

SOFIE. Dusting, sweeping, vacuuming, it fills me with depression.

DR. FRANS. Yes, that is all very normal. One must develop depressing routines in order to recover from tragedy.

SOFIE. Oh.

But.

You see, when I'm depressed...then I think about Wink even more?

(Pause.)

(Perhaps housework is not the answer.)

DR. FRANS. ...Perhaps you should take up a hobby.

For example, I have had patients who achieved a great deal of success with placemats.

There is something very calming about creating a placemat. It says: I am here, I am in my place, all things are in their places.

Yes, perhaps you should make placemats.

SOFIE. *(Emotional.)* Wink would never have used a placemat.

DR. FRANS. *(Sternly.)* You must move on from the cat.

SOFIE. I cannot. I cannot move on from Wink.
All joy and unpredictability has drained from my life since Wink disappeared.

DR. FRANS. "Unpredictability"?

SOFIE. ...Yes?

DR. FRANS. Sofie. I am trying to help you. And you must believe me when I tell you that there is no *joy* in *unpredictability*. You must strive for steadiness in all things. You must take any longing you feel for "unpredictability" and SHOVE IT DOWN.

SOFIE. Shove –?

DR. FRANS. SHOVE IT DOWN.

SOFIE. Shove it...down.

DR. FRANS. SHOVE IT DOWN!

SOFIE. Shove it down!

DR. FRANS. SHOVE IT DOWN!!

SOFIE. SHOVE IT DOWN!

DR. FRANS & SOFIE. SHOVE IT DOWN!!!!

> *(Beat.)*

DR. FRANS. And then you must say to yourself, "I am a woman who has shoved down my reckless and damaging beliefs, and now I am ready to go on vacation."

SOFIE. Vacation?

DR. FRANS. – With Gregor, which we will discuss in more detail next week. See you then!

> (**SOFIE** *gets up to go. In the door:*)

SOFIE. Doctor...?

DR. FRANS. What is it?

SOFIE. What if the thing that I am feeling, as I am buffeted by endless waves of grief and longing, can *not* be shoved down but rather is a sudden awareness of the unspeakable void in my life that must be filled by something else no matter how reckless or dangerous?

(Beat.)

DR. FRANS. That's very unlikely, Sofie.

SOFIE. Oh.

DR. FRANS. Have a good day!

SOFIE. *(Trying to be bright.)* You too!

(She leaves.)

(A beat, in which **DR. FRANS**' *loneliness shows itself to us. It is palpable.)*

4.

(A storm!)

(A light up on **WINK**, *the cat.)*

(He is skinned. Scarred. Tough.)

(Drenched and filthy.)

(The following is entirely in control, self-possessed, almost a seduction.)

WINK. After I was skinned, I was buried in the garden.

After I was buried in the garden, I lay there for a time.

I listened to the soil settle.

I listened to the worms moving through the soil.

It started to rain. I listened to the rain, gentle on the topsoil.

I thought: "It's very calm, being dead."

Then I thought: "It's fine, except that I'm hungry."

Then I thought: "Can I be dead and still be hungry?"

Then I thought: "If I'm hungry, I'm not dead."

Then I thought: "If I'm not dead, then I am...alive."

And the thought went straight through me like the shock of desire.

I sat bolt upright. And the earth gave around me.

And as the rain fell on my furless furious head, I thought: "I didn't want the calm anyway."

Who needs calm when one can have vengeance?

(He studies us.)

(He smiles. It is terrifying.)

And that's how I rose up.

That is how I rose up from the garden...Doctor.

5.

(A light on **SOFIE.***)*

(Alone in the house.)

(She is cleaning, with great purpose. She finds a cat toy under the chair. She holds it. Beat. She [very silently] starts to weep inconsolably.)

(She tears the cat toy to shreds. She tears it and tears it. Catnip everywhere. Shreds everywhere. She steps on its pieces.)

(Beat.)

(She looks at the damage. A warrior is born. She destroys the entire living room with the fervor of someone who has only recently learned that destruction is power. This should go from hilarious to sad to terrifying to maybe hilarious again. There can be multiple movements within the destruction sequence. It is an entire emotional journey.)

(Beat. She surveys the destruction. She returns to her right mind. She is deeply shaken.)

SOFIE. Oh.

Oh no.

(A key in the door. **GREGOR** *enters.)*

GREGOR. My God.

SOFIE. Gregor.

GREGOR. Good lord!

SOFIE. Gregor!

GREGOR. What has happened here, Sofie!

*(***SOFIE** *contemplates telling the truth. Then, before she knows exactly what she's going to do:)*

SOFIE. It was a man, Gregor.

GREGOR. A man?

SOFIE. He...broke in!

GREGOR. A man broke in?

SOFIE. Yes, after I opened the door.

GREGOR. Why did you open the door!

SOFIE. He disguised himself as the postman, and then he ransacked our living room!

GREGOR. What was he looking for?

SOFIE. *(Now she's just winging it.)* The cat!

GREGOR. ...The cat?

SOFIE. He loves cats!

GREGOR. We no longer have a cat!

SOFIE. And...he threw me down on the floor!

> *(Okay now this is getting a little hot for both of them.* **GREGOR** *and* **SOFIE** *are carried by the tide of this fantasy.)*

GREGOR. This is really too much!

SOFIE. He threw me up against the wall!

GREGOR. He might have had his way with you!

SOFIE. His hands on my shoulders, on my neck.

GREGOR. He might have skinned you!

SOFIE. ...Excuse me?

> *(Everything grinds to a halt.)*

GREGOR. I said...we must call the police. Immediately.

SOFIE. ...The police?

GREGOR. Where did he go?

SOFIE. He...
   well
   that is to say
   ...he ran!
   To the back of the house!
   And he threw open the kitchen window, and
   he jumped.
   Out.

GREGOR. We have to track him down.

SOFIE. No no...that's not necessary.

GREGOR. He ransacked my home, he assaulted my wife –

SOFIE. I didn't see him very clearly.

GREGOR. He threw you against a wall, Sofie, how could you not see him clearly?

SOFIE. His hair – it was shaggy.

GREGOR. Yes?

SOFIE. And his face – it was dirty.

GREGOR. Was he tall? Was he short? Was he – in any way –

(Jealous.)

Attractive?

SOFIE. His eyes –

GREGOR. What about them?

SOFIE. They burned straight through me.

The eyes of a madman, or a prophet. Like chips of ice.

GREGOR. Sounds like cataracts to me.

SOFIE. Not cataracts, fervor. And he stared at me with such intensity –

GREGOR. *(Even more jealous.)* Perhaps he was near-sighted.

SOFIE. *(Wistful.)* I was so frightened.

GREGOR. This is unacceptable!

(He storms out of the room.)

*(**SOFIE** stands for a beat in the destroyed living room. She imagines a savage force of uncontrollable destruction – dressed as the postman.)*

SOFIE. Roland.

His name was Roland.

6.

(*Dr. Frans' apartment.*)

(**DR. FRANS** *and* **WINK** *face each other.*)

(**DR. FRANS** *is wide-eyed.*)

(**WINK** *is bedraggled.*)

DR. FRANS. I feel that in good conscience I must tell you that I have never treated a cat before.

WINK. Your sign says "Doctor."

DR. FRANS. My...?

WINK. Right outside, right by the door, it says "Doctor."

DR. FRANS. I'm not that sort of doctor.

WINK. And yet, you'll do, for the moment.

> (*He circles* **DR. FRANS**.)

> (*He leans in, close, and sniffs him.*)

DR. FRANS. Perhaps you'd like some tea.

WINK. Milk.

DR. FRANS. I don't have any milk.

WINK. A blanket.

DR. FRANS. A blanket?

WINK. I would like a blanket.

> (**DR. FRANS** *approaches* **WINK** *with a blanket. He is so rarely this close to another creature. Gingerly, he drapes it over* **WINK**'s *shoulders. A curious beat between them as they take each other in.*)

> (**DR. FRANS** *feels a strange stirring that he's never felt before.*)

DR. FRANS. How did you...[find me]?
That is to say...

WINK. I have smelled you, Doctor Frans. On their hair, their skin, their clothes.

And now here we are.

Face to face.

> (**DR. FRANS** *is shaken by the proximity. He tries to take back control of the situation.*)

DR. FRANS. Sofie rescued you from the street as a kitten, did she not?

WINK. She needed me.

DR. FRANS. Sofie loves you very much.

WINK. She's weak for me. Many women are weak for me.

DR. FRANS. You don't say.

WINK. And men as well, men have been weak for me, in my lifetime.

> (*He gives* **DR. FRANS** *a bold stare.*)

DR. FRANS. Ah...oh.

WINK. (*Glancing around.*) Your home is very large.

DR. FRANS. Ah – yes...well...

WINK. The light. During the day, you must get some light?

DR. FRANS. Yes, I suppose...

WINK. And the painting. Did you do it?

DR. FRANS. I? No. Yes, sort of.

It's paint by numbers.

> (**WINK** *stares at him blankly.*)

Do you paint?

WINK. Me, Doctor?

I hunt and kill.

DR. FRANS. (*Oh my.*) Of course.

> (*Beat.* **WINK** *makes a decision.*)

WINK. It will do.

DR. FRANS. I'm sorry...what will?

WINK. Your place.

For me.

DR. FRANS. Oh...

WINK. To recover.

DR. FRANS. Oh...well...

WINK. It's a little bare. Somewhat depressing. But...

>   *(He shrugs.)*

Options are limited.

>   *(**DR. FRANS**' feelings are hurt by this, even if he tries not to show it.)*

DR. FRANS. Depressing?

WINK. Don't you think?

DR. FRANS. All houses must be depressing, otherwise we would never go to work.

WINK. That may well be the case.

DR. FRANS. And don't you like the painting?

WINK. *(Not mean.)* No.

DR. FRANS. You don't?

WINK. No, not at all.

DR. FRANS. *(Saddened.)* ...Oh.

>   *(**WINK** looks at him. Realizes his feelings are hurt. Isn't sure what to do about this, if anything.)*

WINK. You could make another one.

DR. FRANS. I'm not much of a painter.
I tried to generate a hobby for myself, but I found it difficult.

WINK. A...hobby?

DR. FRANS. An activity that might elicit a feeling of well-being.

WINK. All of my activities are hobbies.

DR. FRANS. That can't be possible.

WINK. Why not?

DR. FRANS. It isn't possible to live that way.

WINK. I eat. It is enjoyable.
I sleep. I feel content.
I hunt, as we discussed, and I feel...exhilarated.

If something did not make me feel good, I simply
wouldn't do it.

DR. FRANS. ...Oh.

> *(Beat.)*

WINK. Is there a bed?

DR. FRANS. There is a...*my* bed...but that's not...

WINK. A bed is a bed, no?

DR. FRANS. To *share* a bed is a thing that...

How long do you think you'll stay?

WINK. Until I've recovered.

DR. FRANS. And then...?

WINK. Ah. Yes. Questions. Let me ask you one of my own.
What do you know of vengeance?

DR. FRANS. *(Alarmed.)* Very little! Next to nothing! A
civilized man does not...would never...not usually...

WINK. Then let me tell you this.

I will stay here, and I will heal, and I will grow stronger.
And when Gregor comes here next, I will skin him
from head to toe.

And that, Doctor, is what we, who are not so civilized,
know as revenge.

DR. FRANS. Wink...

WINK. *(Turns back to* **DR. FRANS**, *smiles.)* But until then, I'll
take the bed.

7.

(Late at night. **SOFIE** *is awake. Outside the bedroom. She tells herself an erotic bedtime story.)*

SOFIE. He breaks through the door.
   With his madman eyes, his madman hands.
   I say, "No!" I say, "What are you doing here."
   A man on a mission of – terror.
   I am terrified, personally.
   He throws me against the wall.
   His eyes – savaging me. Ravaging me.
   He says:

   (Beat – she finds Roland's voice inside her:)

   "I could snap your neck."
   (As herself.) He can. He *can* snap my neck.
   He is a – a –
   A terrorist.

   (This is the best thing she has ever considered.)

   Here. In my house.

   (Quiet thrill.)

   I'll never be safe again. He says:

   (Becomes Roland, with real confidence:)

   "Never again will you be safe."

   (This revelation is a fresh, true draft of power.)

   *(***GREGOR*** appears in the doorway to the bedroom, rumpled with sleep, confused.)*

GREGOR. Sofie? What are you doing?
SOFIE. Nothing.
GREGOR. Come back to bed.
SOFIE. In a minute.

(**GREGOR** *studies her uneasily. There is something new in her that he doesn't know. She studies him as well.*)

Gregor?

GREGOR. Yes.

SOFIE. Are we happy?

GREGOR. Yes.

SOFIE. Are you sure?

GREGOR. Yes.

SOFIE. If we weren't happy, would we know it?

(*Beat.*)

Gregor?

GREGOR. During the day, I go to the office and I work very hard.

During the day, you stay at home and you work very hard.

Every week, we go to see Doctor Frans, who works very hard.

Everybody is working very hard, Sofie.

Doctor Frans says we are doing very well.

If we are working hard at doing very well, we must be happy. Don't you think?

SOFIE. But Wink is gone.

GREGOR. Wink was not working very hard.

SOFIE. But –

GREGOR. Did you ever see Wink working at all? Let alone very hard?

(**SOFIE** *has* not *seen Wink working at all, let alone very hard.*)

SOFIE. I dream about him, sometimes.

I dream that he's lost, or I dream that he's sad, or I dream that he needs me and I can't get to him.

GREGOR. (*Trying to comfort her.*) Wherever he is I'm sure that he's dry, and very happy.

GREGOR. *(Shy.)* Do you ever dream about me?

SOFIE. About you?

GREGOR. About me.

SOFIE. *(Taken aback.)* No, I don't.

GREGOR. Oh.

SOFIE. ...Do *you* dream about *me*?

GREGOR. *(Has to be honest.)* ...I guess not.

SOFIE. Okay. Well.

> (**GREGOR** *makes the choice to try to communicate something elusive and dangerous.*)

GREGOR. Sofie?

SOFIE. What.

GREGOR. Sometimes I have dreams in which I'm doing something I didn't mean to, but it feels so good that I can't stop. Do you ever have those?

SOFIE. *(She definitely does.)* Maybe?

GREGOR. And say, for example, that the thing you're doing is horrible and monstrous. Say, for example, it's the sort of thing that the awake-you would never do. And then say that maybe you *do* do that thing – once, for example. Just one time. No big deal. But *then*...

SOFIE. What thing?

GREGOR. I don't know.

Just for example, I mean.

SOFIE. You must have been thinking of something.

GREGOR. No, nothing. I forget.

> *(Beat.)*

SOFIE. I've been having these dreams recently...?

Or sort of...not dreams, exactly...more like memories... or sort of, not *memories* exactly, but...memories of what *could* happen.

GREGOR. ...*What* could happen?

SOFIE. I don't know, it's hard to say
    sort of just lots of things
    like
    Roland.

GREGOR. Who?

SOFIE. That man, the one who broke in.

GREGOR. You didn't tell me you knew his name!

SOFIE. I guess he mentioned it.

GREGOR. What else did you talk about!

SOFIE. Well, he happens to be a very renowned terrorist.

GREGOR. A terrorist?!

SOFIE. *(With some satisfaction.)* Roland, Roland the Terrorist.
    He's done many terrifying things. We discussed some of them.

   *(**GREGOR**'s outrage is bleeding into intrigue.)*

GREGOR. ...Like what?

SOFIE. Well, he manifested a fire. And he brokered a drought. And he generated a plague.

GREGOR. He mentioned that when he broke in?

SOFIE. No, he wrote me a letter afterwards.
    Roland does a little bit of everything, but he hasn't been ready to specialize just yet.

GREGOR. Did he say that in the letter?

SOFIE. Semaphore.
    With flags.

GREGOR. From where?

SOFIE. A neighboring rooftop.

GREGOR. ...Oh.
    What else did he say?

SOFIE. *(Deeply wistful, something raw and exposed.)* He said he saw something...in me.
    And then he said: Go.

GREGOR. Go?

SOFIE. Just: Go. And then he dropped a stick of dynamite down the chimney.

GREGOR. Down *our* chimney??

SOFIE. It was unlit.

> *(Beat…and she breaks it:)*

Anyway, we should get some sleep.

> *(She turns to go.)*

> *(And **GREGOR** catches her hands.)*

> *(He doesn't know what to do to bring her closer again. Or to bring himself closer. He kisses her. After a moment, gently, she stops the kiss. A moment.)*

GREGOR. Sofie?

SOFIE. *(So gentle.)* Shhh.

Roland is close by. And he can hear everything we're saying, he can hear our blood in every one of our tiny veins, he can hear our skin wrinkle and our eyelids blink, and everything we're thinking, and everything that's in our hearts, and Roland says, "Shhh."

GREGOR. Do you think we can be like we were before?

SOFIE. Roland told me there's no past anymore, there's only future.

GREGOR. Oh.

SOFIE. *(Gentle.)* Goodnight, Gregor.

> *(She exits, back toward the bedroom.)*

> *(Beat.)*

> *(**GREGOR** goes to a loose floorboard. He pulls it up. He brings up a box. He opens it. He holds Wink's fur to his chest.)*

GREGOR. Sometimes I imagine that I am skinning the cat all over again.

Blood on my hands. Blood and fur.

Sometimes at the office, I stare out the window and imagine myself removing sheet after sheet of fur from every animal in the world.

> *(Raw, exposed, wistful. He holds the fur against his cheek.)*

And then sometimes I imagine that I'm the one covered in this.

That there is a layer of skin and hair rendering me – grotesque. Fearless.

> *(Beat – new clarity and conviction:)*

I don't think I can give this up.

8.

(Morning, in Dr. Frans' home office. **DR. FRANS**
*sleeps on his couch, under a thin blanket. He
is in a state of undress.)*

*(***WINK*** *sits bare inches from* **DR. FRANS**,
staring at his face. **WINK** *wears one of the
doctor's bathrobes loosely wrapped around
himself. After a moment,* **WINK** *puts his face
very, very close to* **DR. FRANS**. *He breathes.* **DR.
FRANS** *wakes up with a jolt.)*

DR. FRANS. Ahhh!

WINK. Good morning.

DR. FRANS. What are you doing!

WINK. Watching you.

DR. FRANS. Why!!

WINK. I don't know. I felt like it. Now I'm done. Is there
food?

DR. FRANS. Oh...uh...yes. Food! Yes.

WINK. Good, I would like food now.

DR. FRANS. Oh...of course...

*(He is going to get up...and realizes he's not
fully clothed. And* **WINK** *is still watching
him.)*

Uh...if you'll...excuse me?

(He means: look away.)

*(***WINK*** *either doesn't know or doesn't care.
He is barefoot and disheveled and radiating
careless power.)*

WINK. Why aren't you sleeping in your bed?

DR. FRANS. ...You were there.

WINK. Yes?

DR. FRANS. I couldn't sleep in my bed if you were in my bed.

WINK. Why not?

DR. FRANS. It's not...it's just not the sort of thing one should do.

WINK. I sleep where I want. Shouldn't you?

DR. FRANS. It's complicated.

> *(He is trying to get dressed under the blanket without exposing himself to* **WINK.**)

If you wouldn't mind...?

WINK. Yes?

DR. FRANS. A civilized man requires privacy as he dresses.

> (**WINK** *turns his back briefly – but soon turns back around and watches as* **DR. FRANS** *puts on his clothes.*)

WINK. Have you always worn...clothes under your clothes?

DR. FRANS. Civilized men wear clothes, and clothes under their clothes.

WINK. And what is the purpose of that?

DR. FRANS. Ahh...well...

> *(He isn't quite sure.)*

The purpose, you see, is

that

is how

it is done.

WINK. Your pants seem very constricting.

DR. FRANS. All pants must be constricting. They keep us from running wild.

You're looking.

WINK. Yes, I am.

> *(A beat between them.)*

> (**DR. FRANS** *feels a current he cannot identify and has no idea what is called for.*)

Tell me, Doctor.

On the subject of my breakfast.

DR. FRANS. Ah...breakfast! Go on.

WINK. Is there any meat?

DR. FRANS. Meat?

WINK. Bacon. Pork. Sausage.

DR. FRANS. Uh...no... I don't cook, I'm afraid.

WINK. What about uncooked meat?

DR. FRANS. *(Faint with horror.)* Pardon me?

WINK. Something dead?

Something alive, and struggling a little?

DR. FRANS. Absolutely not!

That is to say...I do not...a man like me would not...

Nothing is struggling in my kitchen.

WINK. What a shame.

DR. FRANS. I could make you toast.

> (**WINK** *gives* **DR. FRANS** *a facial expression that shows what he thinks of toast.*)

...Forget the toast.

WINK. Don't worry, Doctor, I'll provide my own meal.

DR. FRANS. How will you do that?

WINK. You have a back garden, do you not?

DR. FRANS. I, well, yes I do.

> (**WINK** *approaches him, slow, stalking him. A seduction to it, but also a rhythm of the hunt.*)

WINK. Then here is what I will do.

I will go out to your garden.

I will sit in the sun.

Motionless, very still, barely even breathing.

But my eyes, Doctor. They will scan the horizon.

They will see everything.

And sooner or later, something will move.

Some creature, unaware of me.

Just moving through its daily paces, its banal grubbing.

Nose to the grindstone.

And then I will rise to my feet, so silently,
I will slip toward it
closer and closer
so carefully, so silently
it will have no idea I'm even there.
And when I am so close
that I can feel the heat of its flanks
the tiny drum of its desperate heart
then, Doctor
I will pounce.

> *(He makes a sudden motion.)*

> *(Startled,* **DR. FRANS** *recoils, almost tripping.* **WINK** *smiles.)*

Your heart is beating very quickly.

DR. FRANS. Excuse me?

WINK. I can hear it from here.

DR. FRANS. I have a slight – coronary – condition. But it's nothing at all to speak of.

WINK. What a relief to hear. Until after breakfast, Doctor Frans.

> *(He turns to go.)*

DR. FRANS. *(Bursts out.)* I'll cook for you.

WINK. You will?

DR. FRANS. I would prefer that while you are with me...
I would prefer that nothing is murdered in my garden.

WINK. You would rather it be murdered elsewhere, arrive at your door many days after its death, and be cooked until one can no longer taste the lack of freshness?

> *(A moment. And then, sincerely:)*

DR. FRANS. Yes. Yes that is what I would prefer.

> *(...And, to his own surprise,* **WINK** *gives in.)*

WINK. All right, Doctor.
However you wish.

9.

*(**SOFIE** and **DR. FRANS** in a session. **DR. FRANS** is a little more agitated, a little less put together. **SOFIE** lives in her power in a wholly new way.)*

SOFIE. – And also he kicked up a tsunami, and he brought down a flood, and then at one point he blew up Topeka. And there's a severe deforestation that owes itself to him as well. Because the thing about Roland is that he is prolific. His shapes are numerous. He doesn't believe in limitation, and so he is...unlimited.

DR. FRANS. Well, I do think / we're coming to the end of –

SOFIE. He's been lurking around the house – I saw him again this morning, while Gregor slept. I was reading the newspaper, and I looked out the window and I saw a shadow. And then he stepped out into the sun.

DR. FRANS. *(Bursts out.)* I have a new patient today.

SOFIE. Oh?

DR. FRANS. This patient is a very charismatic and troubled young man, and he has come to me for help – so I mustn't go over time.

SOFIE. Roland is also very charismatic and troubled. When he stared back at me, in the incandescent sunlight, I felt – for the first time – as if someone who understood me was staring into my eyes.

DR. FRANS. *(Recognizing this feeling.)* Oh!

SOFIE. Yes?

DR. FRANS. In the sunlight?

SOFIE. In the sunlight.

DR. FRANS. Was he barefoot?

SOFIE. Barefoot?

DR. FRANS. With his hair a little damp from sleep, and his – your – his bathrobe falling open, and –

SOFIE. Are we talking about Roland?

DR. FRANS. Roland, yes of course Roland.

SOFIE. I suppose he might have been a little damp from sleep, but I don't remember that he was wearing a bathrobe. Roland is a powerfully charming man, few can resist him.

DR. FRANS. I am a man to whom such charm means very little. But one of my...friends...is deeply taken with that patient of mine. This friend has discovered a well of adoration and jealousy that he never knew could exist. This friend is a very weak man.

SOFIE. I don't think I would call that weak.

DR. FRANS. You wouldn't?

SOFIE. Your friend must feel a surge of some kind. Like electricity or a high wind, bearing him along.

DR. FRANS. Well I... I'm not sure. Maybe a surge.

SOFIE. Being near Roland is like being caught in a tornado. When he looks into my eyes, I feel myself being transported.

DR. FRANS. But shouldn't one...? That is to say, shouldn't one slam that down?

SOFIE. Oh. No, I don't think so.

DR. FRANS. Oh...

SOFIE. I think one should sort of...lift it up.

DR. FRANS. Lift it up?

SOFIE. Lift it up!

DR. FRANS. Lift it up!

SOFIE. Lift it UP!

DR. FRANS. LIFT IT –

(A sudden thought.)

– he feels very far away.

SOFIE. Roland?

DR. FRANS. No! My patient, my patient.
Sometimes, even when we're in the same room, he feels so impossibly far from me. And then – I hesitate to tell you this but then – a great ache opens in my chest.

(Beat.)

DR. FRANS. Do you remember...when you and Gregor first met...did odd and upsetting shifts occur inside you – without your volition – despite whatever you may have wanted to say or feel or do? And did those shifts completely dishabilitate you? And were you torn between self-hatred and ecstasy? Do you remember?

(**SOFIE** *does remember.*)

(*And the memory shakes her, a little bit.*)

SOFIE. Yes, I... Yes.

DR. FRANS. And what did you do about it?

SOFIE. I married him.

DR. FRANS. And did those feelings, those odd and upsetting – did they go away?

SOFIE. Eventually they went away.

DR. FRANS. And were you relieved?

SOFIE. No, then I was sad. And then I came to you. And you made me feel better.

DR. FRANS. (*Truly asking.*) Did I?

SOFIE. Or you made me feel less, which at the time, I believed would be better.

DR. FRANS. There are moments in which I find myself wishing I could feel less.

I didn't know I was a person who could have that wish.

(*Beat – with quiet honesty:*)

Things won't ever go back to how they were, will they?

SOFIE. I don't think so.

DR. FRANS. What if I'm not ready?

SOFIE. You are. Roland said so.

DR. FRANS. How does Roland know?

SOFIE. He saw it through the smoke
of the raging fire
he's just about to set.

10.

(DR. FRANS and WINK, evening.)

(They sit on the couch together. Music plays on a radio or record player.*)

(There is a heat between them, an interest and awareness. DR. FRANS tops up their wine glasses. Gestures to WINK's bare feet.)

DR. FRANS. Is it...very unconstricted, like that? Without shoes?

WINK. It is.

DR. FRANS. Is it – very nice?

WINK. Yes. I find it nice.

DR. FRANS. *(Wistful.)* Ah...

WINK. You might try it.

DR. FRANS. I could never do that.

Now?

WINK. Why not?

DR. FRANS. One does not – one should never –

WINK. No one's here to see you. No one would ever know.

DR. FRANS. You're here.

WINK. Me, Doctor?

I'm just a cat.

(The heat between them increases. DR. FRANS sits on the couch. Very carefully, he unlaces his shoes. He removes them gingerly, carefully. He sits on the couch, sock-feet raised above the floor.)

Your socks.

DR. FRANS. My socks?

---

*A license to produce *Wink* does not include a performance license for any third-party or copyrighted music. Licensees should create an original composition or use music in the public domain. For further information, please see Music Use Note on page 3.

WINK. Remove them.

DR. FRANS. I – I'm not quite ready.

WINK. All right then.

> (**DR. FRANS** *lowers his sock-feet to the floor.*
> *He sits with his eyes closed. This should feel*
> *intensely intimate, vulnerable. He lets out a*
> *shaky breath.*)

How is it?

DR. FRANS. It is

very…

Frightening.

> (*He opens his eyes. He looks at* **WINK** *– a*
> *searching and vulnerable look.*)

The floor. It is much closer than I ever anticipated.

WINK. Yes.

DR. FRANS. And…warmer. Realer.

WINK. Yes. Things feel very close – and warm – and real. To those like me.

DR. FRANS. How does one – separate one's self?

WINK. One does not. Often.

DR. FRANS. How does one – protect one's self?

WINK. Violently. With violence.

DR. FRANS. So…exposed. So…accessible.

At any moment anything could – alter your life irretrievably.

How do you live like this?

WINK. Tenuously.

DR. FRANS. (*This was not the answer he expected.*) Tenuously?

WINK. – And then it's over.

> (*A moment between them. Intimate. And so,*
> **DR. FRANS** *dares greatly:*)

DR. FRANS. Have you been…happy?

WINK. "Happy"?

DR. FRANS. Here, with me.

WINK. …Yes.

DR. FRANS. *(This means a lot to him.)* Oh.

> *(**WINK** surprises himself with this question:)*

WINK. …And
have you…[been happy]?

DR. FRANS. *(It bursts out of him.)* Oh yes.

WINK. That's strange.

DR. FRANS. Why is it strange?

WINK. You sleep on the couch.
You prepare my food, to which you aren't accustomed.
Generally a forced change in routine does not seem to
make people…happy.

DR. FRANS. *(From the depths of his heart.)* Some changes
are a gift.
To me, you have been a gift.

> *(A moment between them. **WINK** feels things
> that he doesn't understand.)*

WINK. I watch the way you move, Doctor. I watch the way
you sit.
It is very different from the way that I move and sit.
And yet…I find it strangely thrilling.

DR. FRANS. Do you really?

WINK. It's strange to me, and yet, I do.

DR. FRANS. It's not so very complicated, you know. It's quite
simple, the way a man like myself moves and sits. I find
your movements much more…mysterious.

WINK. How is that?

DR. FRANS. When you stand, it looks as if you're coiling
yourself to spring at someone's throat. But me, when
I stand, I am just…standing. Feet planted on the solid
ground of duty.

> *(He stands, to show **WINK**.)*

*(**WINK** stands as well, rakish and fluid, directly across from him. He tries to adjust his standing to mirror **DR. FRANS**. The following sequence is playful – the two are having fun – and there's a spark and seduction to it as well.)*

WINK. Like that?

DR. FRANS. Ah...almost.

WINK. Like this?

DR. FRANS. That's more how I stand, I think, yes.

WINK. It feels...strange.

DR. FRANS. If I were to stand the way you do – and I can't imagine how I'd do that but –

perhaps –

it might look a little like this?

*(He mirrors **WINK**'s usual stance.)*

WINK. *(Amused, enjoying this.)* Don't forget that you have hips.

DR. FRANS. Perhaps more like this?

WINK. Don't forget that you have shoulders.

DR. FRANS. Like this?

WINK. A lift of the chin, it speaks whole languages. A flicker of the eyes...

Don't forget that you have a chin, and eyes.

*(**DR. FRANS** finds it.)*

DR. FRANS. Oh.

This feels

oh.

WINK. Not bad. And when you move, what do you think of?

DR. FRANS. Oh, when I move, I remind myself to be bowed down by the weight of responsibility, and that is all.

*(He walks. **WINK** mimics him. They're laughing, moving with each other, fascinated by each other.)*

WINK. *(Trying to walk like* **DR. FRANS.***)* Oh yes...like this then.

DR. FRANS. *(Trying* **WINK***'s movements in his own body.)* When *you* move, what do you think of?

WINK. Nothing at all.

DR. FRANS. Nothing?

WINK. I keep my mind very alert and very empty, so that whatever is about to happen next
can just
happen.

> *(A moment.)*
>
> *(They've come to a stop.)*
>
> *(They are so close the air between them sparks. Anything could happen. A kiss, even, could happen.)*
>
> *(And then:)*
>
> *(***GREGOR*** bursts in.)*

GREGOR. Doctor Frans, I'm so sorry, I know it's late and we don't have an appointment and it's after hours but –

> *(Comes to a full stop, seeing* **WINK.***)*

Oh!

WINK. *Oh.*

> *(***DR. FRANS*** *is stumbling to do many things at once, not least of which is get his shoes on.)*

DR. FRANS. Gregor!

GREGOR. You have company.

I'm so sorry.

I've never known you to have company?

DR. FRANS. Gregor, this is – this is not the time! How did you get in?

GREGOR. I knocked at the door for some time and then I broke the window in back and I climbed in. And I realize that is irregular behavior, but these are irregular times and I must speak to you.

(**WINK** *is beginning to circle* **GREGOR** *slowly. A circle that is the stalking of a predator – taking in the whole space, taking his time, narrowing the circle.* **GREGOR** *is curious about the company, without realizing that his life is at stake.* **DR. FRANS**, *however, does.*)

DR. FRANS. Gregor, I think you should leave.

WINK. Oh, just a moment.

GREGOR. ...Have we met?

DR. FRANS. I think tomorrow will be a much better time to / discuss –

WINK. Yes. Yes we've met.

(*He keeps a hunter's gaze trained on* **GREGOR**. **GREGOR** *turns in a slow circle to keep* **WINK**'s *eyes, lulled by him, almost hypnotized.*)

GREGOR. You'll have to excuse me – you seem familiar but I can't seem to...

WINK. Can't you?

GREGOR. Was it at a work event, or...?

WINK. No, it wasn't a work event.

DR. FRANS. Gregor, I *strongly* advise –

WINK. Perhaps it was closer to home.

GREGOR. ...I generally have a good memory for faces. Were we in a crowd?

WINK. I seem to remember we were quite alone, you and I. Just the two of us.

GREGOR. Refresh my memory, it feels right on the tip of my...

DR. FRANS. Gregor!

(**GREGOR** *pulls himself together.*)

GREGOR. Doctor, forgive me. This is what I have come to ask. I have thought about everything you said to me, and I have on more than one occasion practiced *slamming* things down, and I have searched for some answer, any kind of answer, and the only one I have found is not one I expected.

And it is not reasonable.

But – more than anything else so far – it feels right.

How can I tell what is reasonable, and what is actually right?

DR. FRANS. *(Uneasy.)* That is a very good question, but I don't / think [this is the time] –

WINK. Go on, Gregor, tell us. What have you found?

> (**GREGOR** *stands up. With great determination, he drops his pants. He is wearing a pair of underwear sewn crudely but painstakingly out of Wink's fur.*)

DR. FRANS & WINK. Oh!

DR. FRANS. Ah!

WINK. Look at that.

GREGOR. The ancient warriors, Doctor Frans, the Greeks and later the Romans, often went to war clad in the skins of animals. The Vikings, Doctor Frans, went to war in the skins of animals. They were not latent homosexuals.

> (**WINK** *is transfixed, staring at his fur.*)

DR. FRANS. The Greeks, Gregor?

GREGOR. Well maybe the Greeks...

DR. FRANS. The Romans, Gregor?

GREGOR. Well maybe the Romans.

DR. FRANS. ...The Vikings?

GREGOR. Even the Vikings?!

> (*As they both consider the potential latent homosexuality of the Vikings,* **WINK** *makes his move. Behind* **GREGOR***, scissors to his throat.*)

WINK. Don't move. I might slip.

DR. FRANS. Wink, no!

GREGOR. ..."Wink"?

WINK. Surprise.

GREGOR. Oh.

WINK. Let's try a different set of questions, Gregor.
How would you like to be peeled like an apple?

> (*Drawing with the scissor blade, lightly:*)

I'd start right here...
And cut down...
and pull to the side, here...and here...
and flay you, piece by piece.
What do you think of that?

> (**DR. FRANS** *sees a side of* **WINK** *that he has never seen before. Or never let himself see. And yet, he meets* **WINK**'s *eyes, a steady gaze.*)

DR. FRANS. This is not who we are.

WINK. On the contrary, it is exactly who I am.

DR. FRANS. But with me, you're different.
And with you, I'm different.

GREGOR. (*A realization.*) Do it.

DR. FRANS. And these differences – they're worth protecting.
Even from ourselves.

WINK. (*Feels the pull of this, but.*) Leave the room, Doctor.
When you come back, I can be different again.

GREGOR. Please do it.

WINK. Excuse me?

GREGOR. It feels like standing in a high wind
close to the edge of something.
It feels so...real.

WINK. Oh, it will be real, all right.
Don't you worry about that.

> (*He might do it – but:*)

DR. FRANS. But everything will be ruined.
Please, Wink. Don't do this.
For me.

> (*Beat.* **WINK** *and* **DR. FRANS** *look at each other across* **GREGOR**'s *body.* **GREGOR**'s *eyes are*

closed, feeling the scissors at his throat. The life of it. The rush.)

*(And then...***WINK*** drops* **GREGOR**. *He crosses away from him. His face is expressionless.)*

GREGOR. *(To* **WINK**.*)* That was it. I think?

Right then – what I felt –

DR. FRANS. I need you to leave now.

GREGOR. You can't help me, Doctor. But –

(He turns to **WINK**, *with hope.* **DR. FRANS** *moves between them.)*

DR. FRANS. I won't ask you again.

(And **GREGOR** *leaves.)*

(A beat between **DR. FRANS** *and* **WINK**.*)*

Thank you.

WINK. The way we eat, the way we stand, the way we move...

The most basic things inside us, Doctor Frans, are so different.

DR. FRANS. Not so! You showed him mercy.

WINK. I did it for you.

Not for him.

DR. FRANS. Then there is one thing, at least, we share.

(He crosses to **WINK**.*)*

You said you were happy.

WINK. Yes.

DR. FRANS. And I told you that I have been...happy.

WINK. You did.

DR. FRANS. Then maybe together we can be happy. For a long long time. Don't you think?

(Beat. **WINK** *is in unfamiliar territory.)*

WINK. I don't know.

11.

(The house. **SOFIE** *has made a full transformation into* **ROLAND**. *She might make a grand entrance. She plays a song.)*

[MUSIC "ROLAND'S SONG"]

SOFIE / ROLAND.
THE NIGHT I CAUSED A PLAGUE OF LOCUSTS
A DUST STORM RAGED AND BLOOD RAIN FELL
HONESTLY, IT SERVED ME WELL
I WAS SATISFIED

THE NIGHT I CAUSED A POLAR VORTEX
TEMP'RATURES DROPPED BELOW
BUNNIES LANGUISHED IN THE SNOW
AND I WAS SATISFIED

ROLAND IS DARK AND DASHING
ROLAND IS A TERRIBLE LAD
ROLAND IS THE WILD WIND LASHING
ROLAND WILL NEVER BE SAD

THE NIGHT I SUMMONED A TSUNAMI
VILLAGES WERE WASHED AWAY
NOTHING PERMANENT CAN STAY!
AND I AM SATISFIED

FEAR IS MY MÉTIER, IT WILL NOT BE MY MASTER
MY FREEDOM IS DISASTER
(AND) DON'T LOOK FOR SOFIE ANYWHERE...
ROLAND WILL OUTLAST HER...

ROLAND IS DARK AND DASHING
ROLAND IS A TERRIBLE LAD
ROLAND IS THE WILD WIND LASHING
ROLAND WILL NEVER BE SAD

*(***GREGOR** *enters, and stops cold.)*

GREGOR. Who's there!

SOFIE / ROLAND. Does the name "Roland" mean anything to you?

(GREGOR takes her in. The Sofie he knew is no longer present. He accepts this. The creature that is ROLAND is vibrant. It draws him in.)

GREGOR. I heard you were in these parts.

SOFIE / ROLAND. Et voila.

GREGOR. *(Trying to host.)* Can I...get you something? A drink, or...?

SOFIE / ROLAND. Oh I don't need to be brought things, I just take what I want.

GREGOR. Oh! Okay.

(Doesn't plan to say this, but can't help it:)

You seem so...happy.

SOFIE / ROLAND. "Happy"?

GREGOR. Content? ...Satisfied?

SOFIE / ROLAND. I can't complain.

(GREGOR opens his mouth – to ask more questions? – but:)

Let me cut to the chase, Gregor.

I have some bad news for you. And I have some good news.

Would you like the bad news or the good news?

GREGOR. The – the good news.

SOFIE / ROLAND. The bad news is that I have skinned your wife.

GREGOR. How was that for her?

SOFIE / ROLAND. I was very thorough and she appreciated that.

Now ask me for the good news.

GREGOR. What's the good news?

SOFIE / ROLAND. The good news is that you have come at the right moment to attend her service. I will be presiding, and I will give a eulogy, and then it will be your turn to give a eulogy.

GREGOR. I don't know what to say.

SOFIE / ROLAND. Just talk about her.

GREGOR. I'm not sure I knew her very well.

SOFIE / ROLAND. You can keep it short.

(*She may light a candle or some incense.*)

Friends, we are gathered here today in the wake of a gruesome and grotesque and urgently necessary skinning. Sofie was a wife. She was a cat-owner. She was an insomniac and a duster, a vacuum-er and a laundry-doer. She owned many dresses that did not look so good on her. She was good at staying very quiet. She had a nice smile, I think. And now she is skinned.

(*To* **GREGOR**.) It's your turn.

GREGOR. Well.

Uh.

Friends.

We are gathered here together

for Sofie.

She was my wife.

(*He pauses.*)

SOFIE / ROLAND. Say something nice about her.

GREGOR. She always did my ironing. And she never threw out the newspaper until I'd read it. And I never knew what she was thinking, but very recently, I imagine that if I had known, I might have liked it.

SOFIE / ROLAND. (*Encouraging.*) Now say something about when you first met.

GREGOR. When I first met her, I liked her eyes.

There was so much mystery in them.

I thought, I could live next to this person every day and still never know what she was thinking. And that was very exciting because I was very young.

But as we got older, it became hard to spend day after day next to so much unknown.

And it got lonelier and lonelier. But maybe also for her. And now she is skinned.

SOFIE / ROLAND. *(Blows out the candle.)* Goodbye Sofie.

GREGOR. Roland?

SOFIE / ROLAND. What is it.

GREGOR. How did you know what to do?

SOFIE / ROLAND. I just figured it out.

GREGOR. What if you skinned me?

> *(Beat. Then:)*

SOFIE / ROLAND. *(Gently.)* I don't really do things for other people anymore.
I think, if you want to be skinned, that's something you have to do for yourself.

12.

(Morning, in Dr. Frans' home. **DR. FRANS** *sleeps on his couch. Guidebooks to foreign towns are scattered all around him.)*

*(**WINK** sits bare inches from him, staring at his face. After a moment, he puts his head on **DR. FRANS'** chest. **DR. FRANS** wakes up with a jolt.)*

DR. FRANS. Wink!

WINK. Good morning.

DR. FRANS. ...What are you doing?

WINK. Reclining.

DR. FRANS. That's nice.

WINK. *(Gesturing to the scattered books.)* What's all this?

DR. FRANS. Oh, I was just doing a little reading...
Mountain towns and...ocean-front campsites and...
I was just thinking perhaps we might go on vacation.

WINK. Vacation?

DR. FRANS. It was just a passing thought, but it might be nice.
Imagine it, the two of us – a cabin high in the mountains, no one else around... And the night sky might be very large, the stars would be very far away...

WINK. Doctor...

DR. FRANS. And if it were cold, there might be a heavy blanket, the sort of blanket we might curl up under. Or if it were hot, we might have a drink in hand, the cool breeze might ruffle your hair.

WINK. Doctor Frans, I'm leaving.

DR. FRANS. Oh...right now?

WINK. Yes.

DR. FRANS. But you haven't had breakfast.

WINK. I caught something out in the garden.

DR. FRANS. ...You did?

WINK. Yes, and I ate it.

DR. FRANS. *(A little faintly.)* Oh.

WINK. Does that upset you?

DR. FRANS. *(Lying.)* No, not at all.

(*A moment.*)

Will you be back for dinner? I was going to make a branzino, I got five different recipes –

WINK. I won't be back for dinner.

DR. FRANS. In time for a nightcap perhaps?

WINK. I won't be back at all.

DR. FRANS. *(Anguished.)* What did I do?

(*Despite himself,* **WINK** *is moved.*)

WINK. Nothing!

Nothing I did not let you do.

DR. FRANS. Then are you angry with me?

WINK. No, on the contrary.

DR. FRANS. Then why are you leaving me?

WINK. Because this is beautiful. And it has been surprising. But it is not sustainable.

DR. FRANS. Of course it is! We have been sustaining it!

Tell me you care for me.

WINK. Please.

DR. FRANS. In whatever way you can care, even if it is not a very great caring, even if you are only capable of lesser, colder emotions, even if you do not *always* care, but only, say, from time to time –

WINK. Frans.

DR. FRANS. If I knew that you cared for me – even the slightest bit –

(**WINK** *brings* **DR. FRANS**' *head down, as if they might kiss. At the last moment* **WINK** *puts his cheek against* **DR. FRANS**' *cheek, very gently.*)

WINK. You are so full of surprises.

DR. FRANS. Then stay.

Or tell me how to change, and I'll change.

WINK. I hunt, I kill, and I find pleasure. That's who I've always been.

But with you...

(*Beat, then:*)

Don't skin me a second time.

(*One more moment.*)

(*And then, very gently, he disengages.*)

(*And is gone.*)

(*And* **DR. FRANS** *mourns.*)

13.

*(Alone, **GREGOR** skins himself.)*

GREGOR. I am forty years old and I ask my wife, "Do you dream about me?" And she says, "No."

...And now that is gone.

I am thirty-five years old and my wife says, "Look I found a cat," and I look in its dirty little face and I say, "Do we need it?" and then she hugs it. We have not touched in years.

...And now that is gone.

I am thirty years old and on my way to the office a man cuts me off and I'm so angry, I want to put my fist through his jaw...but I swallow it back and continue to the office.

...And now that is gone.

I am twenty-five years old, and I never sleep, I never slow down, something is on its way, but I don't know what or when, only that I'm hungry.

...And now that is gone.

I am twenty years old and there is a woman across the room, the curtains are blowing, something shatters, when our bodies collide there is heat and heat and heat.

...But now that is gone.

I was a young man, and I was a teenager, and I was a child, and I was a fetus, and I was a ball of cells, and now I am gone.

14.

(The house. Or perhaps **SOFIE / ROLAND** *might sit up on the roof. There is nothing affected or put-on about her.* **SOFIE / ROLAND** *is simply herself.)*

*(***WINK*** has just joined her. He is himself as well, although there are certain remnants of Dr. Frans' world that he has incorporated into his look.)*

WINK. Roland the Terrorist?

SOFIE / ROLAND. That's what I said.

What do you want?

WINK. I used to live here.

SOFIE / ROLAND. Did you?

WINK. Yes, a long time ago.

SOFIE / ROLAND. I'm not that concerned about ownership, these days.

This house is my base of terrorist operations.

(Studying **WINK.***)*

You seem familiar...

WINK. So do you...

SOFIE / ROLAND. I blew up Topeka. And Pensacola. And Ikea. So you might have heard of me.

And if not, now you have.

(Beat.)

Offer you a drink?

WINK. What do you have?

SOFIE / ROLAND. I kept the wine but I destroyed the glasses.

WINK. I like a nice red more than I used to.

SOFIE / ROLAND. Cheers.

WINK. To you.

*(***SOFIE / ROLAND*** grabs them each a bottle.)*

(They clink and drink.)

So, terrorism. Is there a future in it?

SOFIE / ROLAND. Seems like.

WINK. What are your future plans?

SOFIE / ROLAND. I'm thinking paramilitary.

WINK. Go on.

SOFIE / ROLAND. A small army. My own army.

WINK. That's ambitious.

SOFIE / ROLAND. I'm ambitious.

WINK. Do you have a political agenda?

SOFIE / ROLAND. Just destruction, mostly.

What're your plans?

WINK. Oh, I don't have any just yet.

> *(Looks around the destroyed room.)*

I like what you've done with the place.

SOFIE / ROLAND. Thanks.

WINK. It's counter-intuitive.

SOFIE / ROLAND. Thank you.

> *(A light on **DR. FRANS**, alone. Very carefully, **DR. FRANS** takes off his shoes. Very, very carefully, he removes his socks.)*
>
> *(At the same time, **GREGOR** staggers out into a clearing. His loins are wrapped only in Wink's fur. He is feral. He sniffs the air.)*
>
> *(The energy in the room is hot and taut now.)*

WINK. One might set up target practice in the basement.

SOFIE / ROLAND. And a training hall, in the back.

WINK. And perhaps a fall-out shelter.

SOFIE / ROLAND. And an extra room for the ammo.

WINK. And extra ammo for the room.

SOFIE / ROLAND. And more wine.

WINK. And fake passports.

SOFIE / ROLAND. And anthrax.

WINK. And recruits.

SOFIE / ROLAND. And –

WINK. And –

SOFIE / ROLAND & WINK. And...

> *(A beat between them, electric. Anything could happen.)*
>
> *(Outside,* **GREGOR** *tilts his head back and howls at the moon. It is equal parts joyful and mournful.)*
>
> *(*DR. FRANS *lowers his feet to the floor. Just before his bare feet touch the floor –)*
>
> *(Blackout.)*

End of Play

Roland's Song
(Wink)

Music by Daniel Kluger
Lyrics by Jen Silverman

Rock

The night I caused a plague of lo-

- custs,   a dust___ storm raged

___ and blood rain fell.___   Hon-est-ly, it served me well.

Roland's Song - p.3

Roland's Song - p.4